Around School

Dona Herweck Rice

Publishing Credits

Rachelle Cracchiolo, M.S.Ed., *Publisher*
Conni Medina, M.A.Ed., *Managing Editor*
Nika Fabienke, Ed.D., *Content Director*
Véronique Bos, *Creative Director*
Shaun N. Bernadou, *Art Director*
Carol Huey-Gatewood, M.A.Ed., *Editor*
Valerie Morales, *Associate Editor*
Courtney Roberson, *Senior Graphic Designer*

Image Credits: All images from iStock and/or Shutterstock.

Teacher Created Materials
5301 Oceanus Drive
Huntington Beach, CA 92649-1030
www.tcmpub.com

ISBN 978-1-4938-9810-7

Printed by: 51497
Printed in: Taiwan

to the  school

at the  school

to the 

desk

at the

desk

to the 

rug

at the 

rug

to the 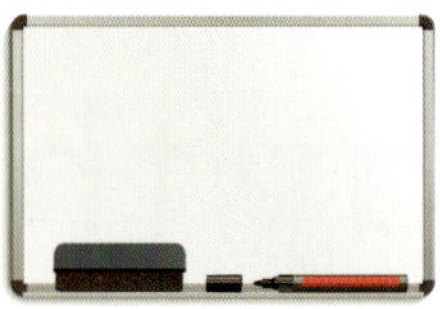

board

at the 

board

to the 

playground

at the 

playground

High-Frequency Words

at
the
to